THE ADVENTURES OF BENNY

Steve Shreve

Marshall Cavendish Children

Marshall Cavendish Corporation, 99 White Plains Road, Tarrytown, NY 10591
www.marshallcavendish.us/kids

Library of Congress Cataloging-in-Publication Data
Shreve, Steve.
The adventures of Benny / by Steve Shreve. — 1st ed.
p. cm.
Summary: A resourceful young boy's adventures introduce him to a host of
characters, including Bigfoot, a mummy, pirates, monkeys,
and his very own Booger-Man.
ISBN 978-0-7614-5575-2
[1. Adventure and adventurers—Fiction. 2. Characters in literature—Fiction.] I.
Title.
PZ7.S559149Adv 2009
[Fic]—dc22
2008054847

The illustrations were rendered in pencil and inked in Photoshop.
Book design by Anahid Hamparian
Editor: Marilyn Mark

Printed in China

First edition
1 3 5 6 4 2

mc Marshall Cavendish
Children

For Benny

Contents

chapter 1

BigFoot

OR

The value of a smelly Friend

Benny woke up early one morning. He packed a baloney sandwich, a fresh pair of underpants, and clean socks—because you never knew when a pair of clean socks or underwear might come in handy.

Benny picked up his fishing pole and lunch basket and headed through the woods to the old fishin' hole.

He walked . . .

. . . and walked . . .

. . . and walked . . .

until he spotted something in
the dirt.

Footprints! And these weren't just
any footprints, but the biggest
footprints Benny had ever seen—
they were even bigger than
his dad's!

*Whoever made these tracks must be
HUMONGOUS*, Benny thought. And
wherever they led, Benny knew it
was sure to be more exciting than
the fishin' hole.

So Benny set off again—this time
to find out where those giant
footprints led.

He was following the strange footprints when suddenly . . .

a great howl rose up from deep inside the forest!

Just then, Benny heard the sound of something crashing through the trees and a shrill cry—"Ouch!"

The cry got louder! "Ouch, ouch!"

And closer! "Ouch, ouch, OUCH!"

And then something came lumbering forward out of the dense, dark underbrush. . . .

"Hi, I'm Bigfoot," said Bigfoot, clutching his butt. He didn't look all that scary, even though he towered over Benny.

"I'm Benny," said Benny. "What were you hollerin' about? Are you okay?"

"I was walking through the woods and sat down on an old log to rest," explained Bigfoot. "Now I've got a big splinter stuck in my hiney, and I can't get it out!"

"Ow," said Benny. "That looks like it hurts. Maybe I can help."

Benny grabbed the splinter and pulled hard, but it wouldn't budge.

He pulled harder, but still—nothing.

Benny planted his feet, got a better grip, and pulled with all his might.

POP!

The splinter came out so fast that both Benny and Bigfoot went flying.

"Thanks a lot," said Bigfoot.

"You're welcome," said Benny. "Say, all of that work made me pretty hungry—do you want to share my baloney sandwich?"

They found a couple of logs (without splinters) and sat down to eat.

Benny looked over at Bigfoot.

"You don't have a nose," said Benny. "How do you smell?"

"Terrible," replied Bigfoot.

"I see," said Benny. "Well, that's a relief. I thought the baloney sandwich had gone bad." He chewed for a moment. "And by the way, don't you get cold running around the forest with no clothes on?"

"Well," said Bigfoot, "my hair keeps me pretty warm. My feet get cold sometimes, though."

Benny opened up his basket and pulled out the extra pair of clean socks he had packed that morning. "Try these on. They're tube socks."

"Wow, these are warm!" said Bigfoot. "I never had a pair of socks before."

"One more thing," Benny said, reaching into the basket.

"Underpants!" exclaimed Bigfoot.

"They might not keep you warm," Benny said, "but they'll help protect you from splinters."

After they finished the baloney sandwich, Benny got ready to leave for the fishin' hole. "It was nice meeting you, Bigfoot," he said.

"You, too, Benny," said Bigfoot. "But before you go, I should warn you—these woods are pretty dangerous. You gotta be really careful."

"Sure," replied Benny. And with that, Benny said good-bye and continued on his way.

It turned out Bigfoot was right. Because up ahead, hiding behind a tree, waiting for Benny to get just a little bit closer was a wolf.

"DINNER!" the wolf snarled as he leaped out from behind the tree.

Benny froze in fear! But only for a second. "Yikes!" he yelled and ran into the woods.

The wolf raced after him—and he was closing in fast! Benny felt the wolf's hot breath on the back of his neck as he got closer, and closer, and closer.

And then the wolf snatched Benny up!

He popped Benny into an itchy burlap sack and threw it over his shoulder.

"Hey!" shouted Benny. "Where are you taking me?"

"To my cave deep in the woods," said the wolf.

"What for?" asked Benny.

"I'm making stew," replied the wolf. "And my sensitive nose tells me you'd make the perfect addition. You smell just like baloney—my favorite."

When they arrived at the wolf's cave, the wolf dumped Benny into a big pot of water.

The wolf added celery, carrots, a potato, half an onion, two cloves of garlic, and a little salt and pepper.

"You stay right there," the wolf said. "I'm going out back to get some firewood so we can get cooking."

But when the big, bad wolf reached the cave's entrance, something was blocking the way.

Bigfoot!

"Hey, wolf," said Bigfoot. "I've got something for you!"

WHAP! Bigfoot's right sock hit the wolf square in the face.

"Oh gross!" cried the wolf. "It smells like . . . Gorgonzola cheese!"

Even though Bigfoot had only been wearing the socks a little while, he did have very smelly feet.

And, as the wolf said, he had a *sensitive* nose.

Before the wolf could recover, Bigfoot's left sock struck the wolf. **WHAP!**

"BLEEARGH!" cried the wolf. "Too . . . stinky. Can't . . . breathe—everything . . . going dark."

The wolf held his nose, staggered back a few steps, and passed out.

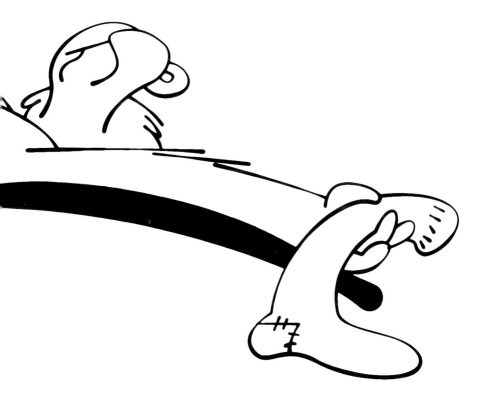

"Thanks, Bigfoot!" said Benny, climbing out of the pot. "Sorry about your new socks, though."

"That's okay," replied Bigfoot. "They were a little itchy anyway. So, are you still going fishing?"

"I'm afraid I lost my fishing pole when the wolf caught me," Benny said.

"Maybe I can help you find it," Bigfoot offered.

"That's OK, I'm saving up for a new one anyway—and it's getting late."

Benny shook Bigfoot's hand and said good-bye. And this time he was *extra* careful as he walked through the woods.

chapter 2

THE MUMMY

OR

ANOTHER GREAT USE FOR TOILET PAPER

Benny's trip to Egypt was a long one. He had traveled by plane, train, two buses, and was now riding a smelly old camel with bad breath into the desert. He couldn't wait to help his uncle Howard, an archaeologist, excavate a mummy for the local museum back home.

When Benny finally arrived, he hopped off the camel. "Hi, Uncle Howard."

"Benny!" his uncle called out. "I hope you're ready to get to work!"

"Work?" Benny asked.

"Work," answered Uncle Howard.

Uncle Howard wasted no time in loading Benny up with a big backpack full of heavy excavation gear—shovels, a pickax, a crowbar, rope, and a roll of toilet paper, because you never know when a roll of toilet paper might come in handy.

Soon, Benny found himself trudging off into the hot desert in search of an ancient pyramid.

After many hours of walking, they came
to a stop.

"Here we are!" bellowed Uncle Howard.

"This is it?" Benny asked. "It's not very big."

"Don't let looks deceive you," replied
his uncle.

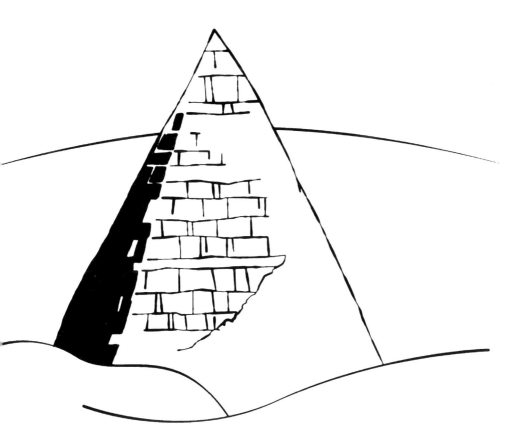

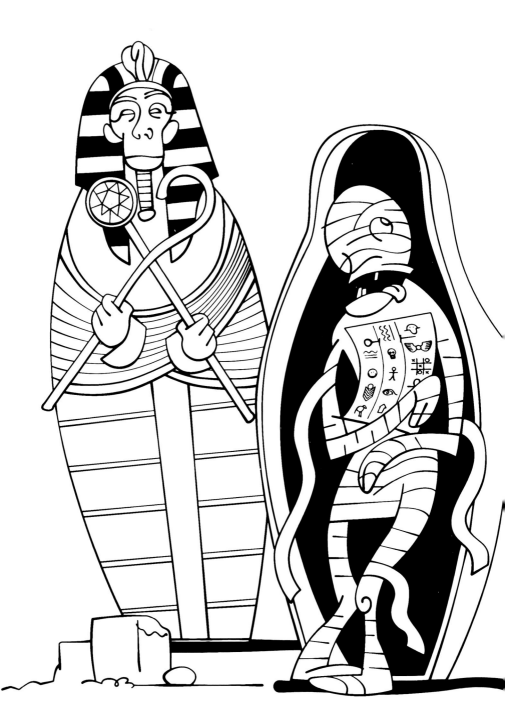

Benny helped his uncle pry open the stone door with the crowbar, and they stepped into the darkness.

Uncle Howard turned on a flashlight and led them down a flight of stairs. He swung the light around the basement room until it settled on a sarcophagus in the corner. Uncle Howard lifted the heavy lid and moved it to the side.

"Eureka! We have discovered the long-lost tomb of King Butthankhamen," Uncle Howard announced. "Better known to the world as King Butt!"

"He looks like a King Butt," Benny agreed. "Hey—what's that pinned to his chest?"

"I say! It looks like some sort of note," said Uncle Howard.

Uncle Howard unpinned the note and explained that is was written in ancient hieroglyphics. He began to decipher the message.

"Beware!" he read. "Whoever disturbs this tomb will invoke the wrath of King Butthankhamen and be cursed to—"

Uncle Howard stopped.

"Cursed?" Benny shouted. "Cursed to what?"

"I can't tell," his uncle replied. "There's some sort of large, brown stain covering the rest."

"Blecch," said Benny. "It's not his brains, is it? I heard they used to pull a mummy's brains out through his nose when they were mummifying him."

"Don't be silly," Uncle Howard said. "His brains are in that jar over there. It's probably just his spleen or something."

"Oh," said Benny. "That's not *so* bad, I guess."

Suddenly, the door at the top of the stairs closed with a great **CRASH!**

"Oh, bother," said Uncle Howard. "I do believe we're trapped."

"It's the curse!" said Benny.

"Nonsense," said Uncle Howard. "There's no such thing as a—"

Uncle Howard was cut off by a scraping sound behind them. Together, they *slooowly* turned around.

"Gadzooks!" exclaimed Uncle
Howard. "It's the mummy!"

King Butt staggered forward.

"Run, Benny!" Uncle Howard cried.

Benny ran, but with the exit sealed, there was no hope of escape.

If I can't get out, Benny thought, *I'll have to stop that mummy.*

Benny ran up behind King Butt, grabbed a loose bandage, and tied it to a large piece of fallen stone.

But Benny hadn't counted on the mummy's strength.

The large rock didn't even slow King Butt down. He just kept moving toward Uncle Howard as his bandages began to unravel.

Then, Benny got an even better idea.

"Hey!" Benny yelled. "Your shoelace is untied!"

King Butt looked down.

Benny and his uncle Howard sprinted down the tunnel—farther into the pyramid.

They ran through a maze of corridors
and stopped to rest around a bend.

"I don't hear anything," Benny noted.
"Maybe he left."

They carefully peeked around
the corner.

The mummy was still far away, but he
was slowly moving toward them.

"Wow," said Benny. "I thought he'd
be faster."

"He is four thousand years old, you
know," replied Uncle Howard. "But . . .
he'll catch up eventually."

"So what do we do now?" asked Benny.

Uncle Howard looked around. "Quick—
into this little room," he ordered.

They went into a room off the corridor
and quietly pulled the door closed
behind them.

"It sure is dark in here," Benny observed.

Uncle Howard lit a match. "Not to worry you," he said, "but we're not alone in this room."

Benny looked around. "Aaah!" he shouted. **"Snakes!"**

They started back toward the door, but it was too late—they heard a noise outside.

"Now what?" asked Benny. "King Butt has caught up to us!"

"Oh, I wouldn't worry too much about him," said Uncle Howard. "The snakes will probably finish us off long before he gets in."

Fortunately, most of the snakes weren't poisonous. Keeping the snakes from crawling into their socks was the worst Benny and his uncle Howard had to deal with.

After a while, they even stopped worrying about King Butt. The mummy was so busy pushing on the door to get in that he never thought to try pulling it.

Benny and his uncle had one new problem, though—after all of that running, they were starting to feel a little hungry.

"You know," said Benny, "maybe we could solve our hunger problem *and* keep those pesky snakes out of our socks."

"What do you mean?" asked Uncle Howard.

"Let's build a fire and cook 'em!"

"Great idea, Benny, my boy," said Uncle Howard. He pulled a box of matches out of his shirt pocket.

It wasn't too long before they were enjoying a nice, hot snake dinner.

"Not too bad, once you get used to the taste," said Uncle Howard.

"And the chewiness," added Benny.

After a few more snakes, Benny and his uncle Howard were starting to feel at home. But just as they got comfortable, they heard King Butt *pulling* the door open.

"Uh-oh," said Benny.

King Butt entered the small room. He was almost completely unraveled now and didn't look too happy about it.

"This is it," said Uncle Howard. "I'm afraid it's the curse for us."

"Oh, well. We were almost out of snakes anyway," said Benny.

Step by plodding step, the mummy drew closer.

Benny could barely watch as King Butt approached him. Then the mummy reached out, grabbed his underpants, and YANKED!

"Aaaah!" Benny yelled. **"Wedgie!"**

Uncle Howard was no luckier. "My underpants!" he bellowed.

The curse now fulfilled, King Butt just
stood there.

"What do we do now?" said Benny.

"I don't know," replied his uncle.
"The museum will never stand for an
unraveled mummy."

"Yeah," agreed Benny. "He looks like a
piece of beef jerky."

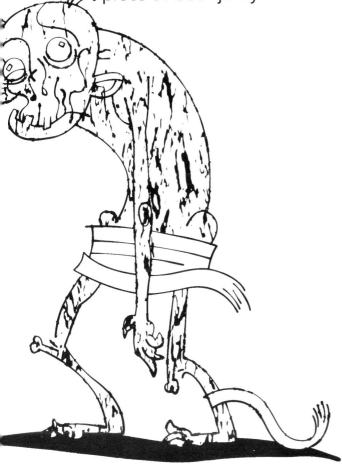

Benny and Uncle Howard tried their best to rewrap King Butthankhamen, but it was no use—his bandages were completely ruined.

"We'll have to bring him like this," said Uncle Howard with a sigh.

"Wait a minute," Benny said, "didn't we pack a roll of toilet paper before we left?"

Uncle Howard considered this for a moment. "It's worth a try, I suppose."

Benny and his uncle quickly wrapped
King Butt in toilet paper and bundled
him off to the airport.

There wasn't much to do on the long
flight, so Benny tried to chat with King
Butt. But unfortunately, mummies
aren't really great conversationalists.

Finally, Benny and his uncle Howard arrived at the museum and dropped off King Butt.

The curator looked at the mummy strangely, but he didn't say anything.

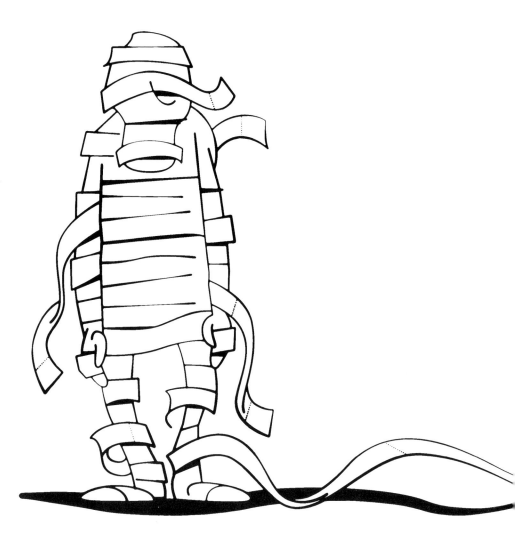

Benny had just one more thing he had to do before going home.

He tore a long piece of toilet paper off King Butt and headed toward the bathroom.

chapter 3

Pirates

OR

The Truth

about Life on

the High Seas

One Tuesday morning, when Benny should have been at school and his father should have been at work, the two of them were driving around in the family station wagon.

"Hey, Dad. Where are we going?" Benny asked.

"Down to Dead Man's Wharf," his father replied. "I thought maybe we'd go deep-sea fishing."

"Really?"

"Yep. I got a coupon," his father said.

Benny was so excited that as soon as his
father parked the car, he jumped out and
ran down to the dock. But what he saw
was a great, four-masted galleon.

As his father caught up, a mean-looking
man with a gold tooth and a hook in
place of his left hand walked over and
introduced himself.

"Arrgh! I'm Captain Long John Underwear! Scourge of the Seven Seas and three of the Great Lakes! What d'ye want?"

"We're here to go fishing," said Benny.

"Here's my coupon," said his father.

"Oh, I'll take ye, but you'll have to work on the voyage—me cabin boy jumped ship when we made port in Cleveland last week, and I be needin' all the help I can get."

"Aww, man," Benny complained.

"Do we get a better discount then?" asked his father.

The captain ignored him.

"Come on then and meet me crew,"
said the captain.

Benny and his father followed
Captain Long John Underwear up the
gangplank and onto the ship.

"This is me first mate, Handsome Francis,
and me second mate, Gunpowder Pete,"
said the captain.

"Welcome aboard, mateys," said
Handsome Francis.

"Arrgh!" said Gunpowder Pete.

"Hoist anchor!" ordered the captain. "Batten the hatches! Raise the mains'l!"

"Aye, aye, Cap'n!" replied Francis and Pete.

"I don't feel so good," said Benny's father, looking green.

Benny turned to Captain Long John Underwear. "Say, what are we fishing for? Tuna? Swordfish? Shark?"

"We're after the most elusive, wily, dangerous creature that ever swam these waters!" replied the captain. "The Great Man-Eating Killer Squid!"

"Why?" asked Benny.

"We can sell the ink to the ballpoint pen factory for a pretty profit," explained the captain. "And after we squeeze out the ink, you and your father can take home all the squid you can eat."

Hearing this, Benny's father leaned over the railing and groaned.

"Now, get to work, you," ordered the captain.

Benny began his chores as the new cabin boy. Somehow, it wasn't nearly as glamorous as he thought it would be.

He did the laundry . . .

and cleaned the loo . . .

and swabbed the poop deck . . .

and cooked the meals.

Later that day, as Benny fried up a nice, plump rat for lunch, first mate Handsome Francis raised the alarm.

"Squid ho!" he shouted from the crow's nest. "Squid off the port bow!"

Benny ran up on deck. At first he didn't see anything. Then, off to his left, a gigantic, suction-cup-covered tentacle rose up out of the dark water. Then another tentacle. And another. And then some more tentacles.

And there it was—the Great Man-Eating Killer Squid!

"Man, that's a big squid," said Handsome Francis.

"That's a lot of ink," said Gunpowder Pete.

"That's a lot of money we'll get for selling it to the ballpoint pen factory," said Captain Long John Underwear.

Just then, the Great Man-Eating
Killer Squid grabbed the ship in
its powerful tentacles and began
pulling it down into the briny deep.

"C'mon, mates!" yelled the
captain. "Man the harpoons!
Ready the cannon!"

Handsome Francis grabbed a harpoon and prepared to spear the killer squid. He tied a heavy rope to the harpoon, took aim, and threw it as hard as he could.

But in his haste, Handsome Francis got his foot tangled in the rope and threw himself overboard, missing the squid completely.

Meanwhile, on the other side of the quickly sinking ship, second mate Gunpowder Pete loaded a six-pounder into the ship's cannon.

"Fire!" ordered the captain.

Gunpowder Pete lit the fuse.

BLAM! The cannon exploded with a deafening roar.

But the cannonball never left the cannon—it was stuck halfway up the barrel.

"I guess I should clean the cannon more often," said Gunpowder Pete.

"Well, there's only one way to handle this now," said Captain Long John Underwear as he picked up a hammer. "The good old-fashioned way!"

The captain bounded over the railing and onto the back of the Great Man-Eating Killer Squid as the ship disappeared beneath the waves.

Benny, who had wisely read all of the ship's safety instructions (because you never knew when they might come in handy), and his father were already in the lifeboat as the ship was dragged down to Davy Jones' Locker.

Before long, they were back on dry land and walking across the parking lot toward the car.

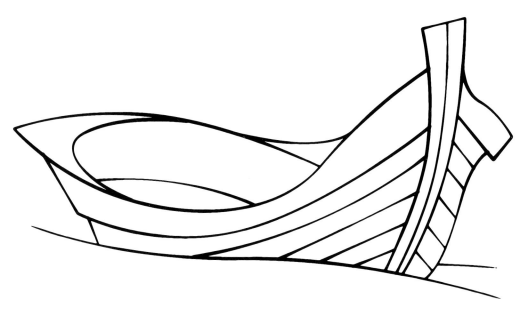

"What a great fishing trip!"
exclaimed Benny. "Can we go
again sometime?"

"I don't see why not," said his father.

chapter 4

THE BOOGER-MAN

OR
A GOOD ARGUMENT FOR NOT PICKING YOUR NOSE

It was late one Thursday night, and everyone was getting ready for bed. Everyone except for Benny—he hated bedtime.

Benny ran around the house in his underwear, as his poor, exhausted father chased him with his toothbrush.

But after awhile, even Benny became tired. So he brushed his teeth, put on his pajamas, and went to the kitchen to feed his dog, Banjo.

They were out of dog food, so
Benny fed Banjo some leftover
hotdogs and sauerkraut he found at
the back of the refrigerator.

Banjo didn't seem to mind.

Finally, Benny climbed into bed, turned out the lights, pulled up the covers, and fell fast asleep.

But later, a loud noise woke him right up—**BANG!**

What's that? he wondered. Benny went to check it out.

He looked in his closet.

He looked in his toy chest.

He even looked through the big, stinky pile
of dirty clothes in the corner.

Well, he thought, *I've checked just about everywhere. Everywhere but under my bed.*

He tiptoed across the room, bent down, and *slooowly* lifted up the covers.

Benny jumped back!

A slimy, bug-eyed monster
leaped out.

"BLEEARGH!" he roared. "I'm
the Booger-Man! And now that
you've found me, I'm going to
eat you!"

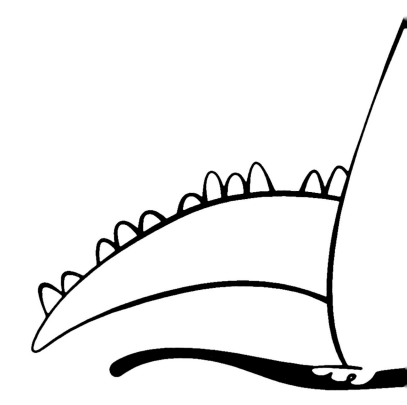

"The Booger-Man?" Benny asked. "I thought it was the Boogey-Man."

"No, that's another guy," the Booger-Man explained. "He lives in Brookfield."

"Wait a minute," said Benny. "What are you doing under my bed, anyway?"

"Hey, I just go where the boogers are—
and someone's been wiping a lot of them
under this bed. Besides, I need a place to
make phone calls, take naps, and do
my laundry."

"I never really thought about all that
before," said Benny.

"Yeah, well, a lot of nose-pickers like you
don't," the Booger-Man replied. "Now
hold still so I can eat you."

"Well, you *could* eat me," said Benny, thinking fast, "but I am pretty little."

The Booger-Man looked closely at Benny. "Hmmm," he said. "You are a bit small."

"But my dog's big and fat," Benny added. "And he never exercises, so he's probably good and tender."

"I suppose that would be okay," said the Booger-Man. "I only had a light lunch, and I am *very* hungry."

So the Booger-Man crept into the living room, where Benny's dog, Banjo, was snoring loudly.

The Booger-Man quietly snuck up behind Banjo. He opened his mouth as wide as he could and prepared to gobble up the dog in one big, boogery bite.

But just then, a tiny little noise came out of Banjo—"poot."

"What's that . . ."

"... horrible, horrible smell?"

cried the Booger-Man.

Banjo had just farted.

"PEE-YEW! What have you been feeding that dog?"

"Hot dogs," replied Benny, "with sauerkraut."

The Booger-Man tried to get away from the stink, but it was too late. His eyes began to water, and his stomach began to heave.

"I think I'm going to be sick!" And with that, the Booger-Man raced for the door . . .

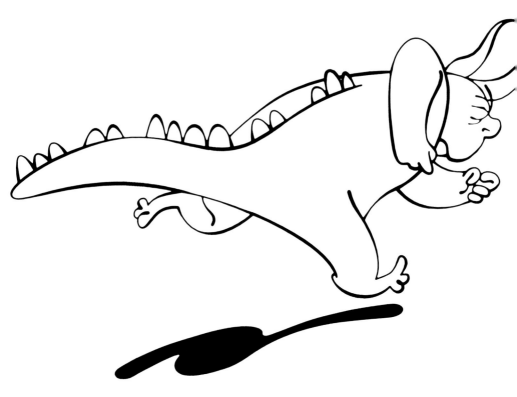

. . . and straight for the bathroom.

He leaned over the toilet . . .

. . . and Benny took this opportunity to sneak up behind him, push him in, and pull the handle——
WHOOSH!
The Booger-Man was sucked head-first down into the sewer system.

Benny always knew that the toilet would come in handy one day.

Benny headed back to his bedroom.

But before going to sleep, he took a few minutes to clean up under his bed.

Just in case.

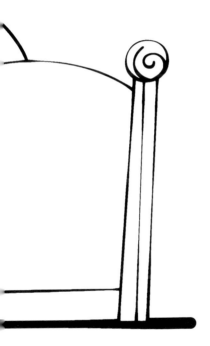

chapter 5

Monkey Island

or

The Advantage of opposable Thumbs

As usual, Benny was wide awake before anyone else one Saturday morning. He rummaged around in his toy chest, looking for something quiet to play with.

Benny reached the very bottom of the chest. "Hey, it's the treasure map! I've been looking for this everywhere!"

Benny had gotten the map in a box of cereal—it led to the treasure of Monkey Island. Since he had nothing better to do this morning . . .

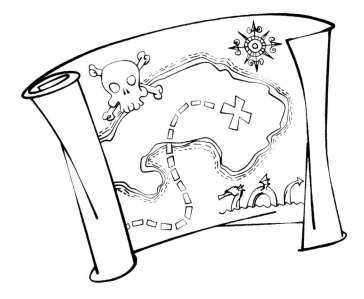

The journey started by boat, so Benny headed down to the pier, where his father kept a little rowboat. He carefully untied it and began to row due east as the map directed.

All of that rowing was very tiring, and just when he was about to give up, a dark silhouette of trees rose up out of the early morning fog.

Benny couldn't believe it. He had reached Monkey Island!

Benny landed the boat on the beach and tied it to a coconut tree.

He pulled the treasure map out of his pocket. "According to this map, I need to walk one-thousand, nine-hundred, and sixty-seven paces due south, right through that dark, scary-looking jungle over there."

So Benny set off through the jungle to find the lost treasure of Monkey Island.

But he had no idea that he was being watched.

Benny counted his paces as he walked. "Nine-hundred and forty-two, nine-hundred and forty-three, nine-hundred and forty-four . . . "

WHAM! A bamboo cage crashed down on top of him. It was a trap!

"Hey, let me out of here!" Benny yelled.

He heard a rustling in the underbrush. The giant tropical fern leaves parted and out of the dark jungle came . . .

. . . the monkeys of Monkey Island!

The littlest monkey stepped forward. "Sorry about that," he said, looking Benny over. "We thought you were somebody else."

As the monkeys freed Benny from the bamboo cage, the little monkey added, "I'm Lenny, by the way."

"I'm Benny. This trap is pretty clever. How did you monkeys build it?"

"We do have opposable thumbs, you know."

"Ah, right," said Benny. "But why do you need to set traps in the first place?"

"We're not the only ones on the island," explained Lenny.

"Who else is here?" asked Benny.

"Well, we've never actually seen anybody, but someone has been sneaking into our village at night and stealing our bananas." Lenny paused. "And then there's the ghost . . ."

Benny gulped. "G-g-ghost?"

"Yep. We've seen him down that way." Lenny pointed to a particularly dark and scary-looking part of the jungle.

"Can you show me on this map?" asked Benny.

"Let's see," said Lenny. "He haunts this part of the jungle here." He pointed at a spot near the X on the map.

"That's where the lost treasure of Monkey Island is," said Benny. "That's what I came here for."

"Well, I should warn you: they say the ghost is guarding the treasure. I'd better go with you," said Lenny. "It's the least I can do after capturing you in that cage."

So Benny and Lenny headed into the haunted jungle.

Lenny brought along a shovel, because you never knew when a good shovel might come in handy. Benny counted off their paces from where he had left off.

"Nine-hundred and forty-five, nine-hundred and forty-six, nine-hundred and forty-seven, nine-hundred and forty-eight . . ."

. . . one-thousand, nine-hundred, and sixty-five; one-thousand, nine-hundred, and sixty-six; one-thousand, nine-hundred, and sixty-seven. That's it!" said Benny. "We should stop and dig here."

Lenny lifted the shovel and began to dig.

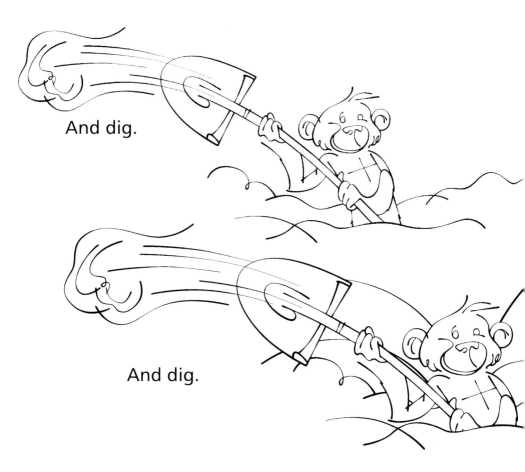

And dig.

And dig.

Until finally, the shovel hit something hard.

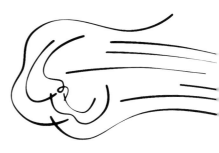

It was a treasure chest!

Benny and Lenny broke the lock with a rock and lifted the lid. The chest was filled with pirate booty: gold doubloons, pearls, diamonds, and rubies.

"Wow!" said Benny. "We're rich!"

"Hot dog!" said Lenny.

But suddenly the ghost jumped out from behind the bushes.

"Aaah! Ghost!" they yelled.

"Woooh!" the ghost moaned. "I am the spirit that guards the treasure of Monkey Island! Leave now or face the consequences!"

"What kind of consequences?" asked Benny.

"I'll give you a wet willie," replied the ghost.

"Aaah! Wet willie!" hollered Benny. "Let's beat it!"

Benny and Lenny turned and ran.

"Woooh!" moaned the ghost,
close behind.

With a nod at Lenny, Benny dodged to
the right around a coconut tree.

Lenny sprinted off to the left and
came up behind the ghost . . .

. . . and hit him in the fanny with the shovel!

"Ouch!" yelled the ghost. "That smarts."

He stood up, and the sheet he was wearing
fell to the ground—he wasn't a ghost at all!

"Now you know my secret," said the fake ghost.

"I knew you weren't a real ghost," said Lenny. "Ghosts don't wear glasses. And I bet you're the one who's been stealing all our bananas."

"Who are you anyway?" asked Benny. "And why were you trying to scare us?"

"I'm Larry. I've been searching for that treasure for forty years. I came up with the ghost story to scare off anybody else who came looking for it."

"Why couldn't you find the treasure sooner?" asked Benny. "Didn't you have the map from the cereal box?"

"I did," said Larry, "but I ran out of toilet paper my first night here on the island."

"Oh," replied Benny.

Benny sat down to think. Larry seemed like a good guy, and he *had* spent a lot of time searching for the treasure. But the treasure was buried on the island where the monkeys lived, and Benny was the one who had the map.

In the end, Benny decided to split the pirate booty evenly with Larry and the monkeys.

And with that, Benny said good-bye
to Larry and the really happy monkeys
and headed back through the jungle to
his little boat.

As he walked, Benny looked at the
gold doubloons and jewels he carried.

Hey, he thought, *I bet I finally have
enough money to buy that new fishing
pole. Sweet.*